KODA

A Story of the First Ancient Native Americans

BY DANNY LESLEY

Dorrance Publishing Co
585 Alpha Drive
Suite 103
Pittsburgh, PA 15238
Visit our website at *www.dorrancebookstore.com*

ISBN: 978-1-6393-7468-7
eISBN: 978-1-6393-7521-9

KODA

A Story of the First Ancient Native Americans

TO HONOR

TO GIVE GLORY

TO OUR LORD GOD

CHAPTER ONE

The Storyteller

Baylor Middleton, is a professor of Early American History, at Ohio State University. Professor Middleton begins the first day of class with the same single question. Each fall semester for twenty-five years introducing himself to class, is followed by "who can tell us when America was discovered?" Immediately, excited young freshman hands reach high, waving to answer. Professor Middleton will point and allow each raised hand to give their answer. Most, not all, respond 1492, Christopher Columbus, or Pilgrims, or *Mayflower* 1620. And some answer Vikings around 1000 AD. Professor Middleton will remind the class, "The question was when, not who. This semester we will study who and when."

Baylor Middleton was born and raised near Jackson, Wyoming. Baylor attended and received an undergraduate degree at the University of North Dakota. From there he went on to Ohio State University receiving his Masters and PhD in American History. Baylor's thesis was Ancient People of Native America.

As a young boy Baylor's mother told stories told her by a grandmother. Those stories were passed down from a great-great-grandfather. In the year 1840, a Cheyenne Native American girl (Winter Sky) became the wife of Garland Baylor, trapper and fur trader. During years of traveling the rivers of the plains, the mountains of Wyoming and Montana, Garland and Winter Sky lived with the people of Crow, Lakota, Pawnee, and Cheyenne tribes. As a young girl, Winter Sky listened to stories of ancient people who were the ancestors of all native human people. She and Garland were told stories passed down through ages of generations of the ancient ancestors. Tales of their bravery, hunting skills, and journeys from faraway homelands.

These stories were told to them by the elders of the various tribes. Elders told of the ancients honoring and respect of the wildlife, the forest, and gifts of food and shelter provided by nature. Eventually settling in the Wyoming territory of 1860s, Garland and Winter Sky came to raising horses and cattle. Winter Sky passed down to her children the stories of her people's ancestors and history. And from there the historic stories that had passed down through the ages of those ancient peoples continued to be told. How the ancient human people found a vast land of bison, rivers, blue sky, and snowcapped mountains.

Baylor grew up hearing those stories. He was raised on family land that had once belonged to the Cheyenne people and their ancestors for hundreds if not thousands of years. Baylor has gone forward teaching history to include the ancient land known as America. He believes all should embrace Native American ancient ancestors as discovering this land.

CHAPTER TWO
Beginnings

For thousands of years an ancient ice age of frigid, icy climate surrounded most of the Northern Hemisphere. Great glaciers grew and crept southward through the Northern lands. North America, including large areas of what is now Alaska, Canada, and America. These glaciers and ice shelf had frozen rivers, streams, lakes, and the seas. As sea levels of the great oceans lowered, what was the sea floor was exposed and grew in size. Over centuries this frozen land became an icy land bridge between north eastern Eurasia, Siberia, and the North America Continent. This frigid land was known as Beringia.

The cooling ice age created natural environmental conditions that could no longer support the great numbers of large mammals of the time. Beginning 18,000 years ago over hundreds of years great numbers of these surviving land animals migrated from Siberia across Beringia in search of new grazing lands. As the mammoth, musk ox, caribou, and others crossed, they were followed by the great predators. The carnivores, nature's apathetic ability to provide an orderly balance of life, death, and survival.

The pack hunting wolves, cave lions, ice bears, and land bears were the largest of predators that reigned over ice age. These deadly predators were closely followed by an even fiercer hunter. The early North American man.

At the ending of the ice age 15,000 years ago, people who had hunted and gathered, had survived across Eurasian for thousands of years, developing hunting skills in creating tools of sharpened bone and stone for spearing. Chipping and shaping rock, and flint into cutting, scraping along with skinning tools. Growing these skills and toolmaking over generations into hunting larger mammals for food and clothing. People developed techniques of hunting in small groups. Skills to stampede and entrap the largest of mammals. Throughout the generations, using skins and hides of hunted animals, they evolved the making of clothing and footwear to protect themselves from the frigid and changing climate. They used small animal bone and sinew for needles and sewn binding material, using skins and hides for fashioning leggings and body coverings. These people of young and old, inquisitive, explorers, skilled hunters, trappers, and fisherman were following the large animal migration across the Beringia Bridge seeking new lands.

These were an intelligent, problem-solving people. They would lead the path opening to North America. This is the story of the ancient ancestors of a people who would live and hunt the prairies of the great plains, live in the mountains dividing east from west, people who would live along the great rivers. A people to be among the great tribes who were the first native Americans—custodians of the land and wildlife.

CHAPTER THREE
Ice Hunt

Crow's small family group of five had been a larger group of hunters and gatherers. Over time Crow had taken in other small hunter family groups. Crow's territory at that time had an abundance of water, animals, and other food sources. As the climate changed, food sources dwindled, mammals began to move, and the hunters followed. Soon Crow found he was sharing his territory with a small tribe of outside hunters. This led to competition over fewer animals to hunt for Crow's family. Eventually the hunters of his band began to move south. Crow's band of five family also included a herd-raised reindeer from Siberia used as a pack animal, and a mature male wolf (Keme), raised from a pup by Crow.

As the ice age was beginning to lessen, glaciers and ice continued to grip much of Northern America and Canada. Areas of east Siberia and western Alaska were a frigid and snowy land inhabited by mammals of the mega-fauna era.

Crow, the leader of a small band of five family members had traveled eastward from east Siberia. Crow and his two sons, as great hunters, would follow the extensive mammals' movement to the grasslands of Alaska.

Cree and Coman were the sons of Crow. Koda, the son of Cree and Pawee, Cree's heart mate (wife). This was the family of Crow. Cree and Coman were brave hunters, providing wild game for the family. As they continued across the Beringia Land Bridge, the sea to the North was partially frozen and offered a barren and fish-enriched water habitat for walrus and seals. The seals were hunted for their blubber, fat enriched meat, and skins. Seal skins were extremely resistant to the frigid cold, water, and constant cold winds. Seal skins were used for clothing and covering for huts and shelters. The meat and fat of the seal gave much needed energy for life in such a climate. Hunting on the ice packs and in need of warming fire, hunters used seal fat and walrus blubber as a primary source of fuel.

Cree and Coman prepared for a seal hunt on the northern ice shelf. Cree had learned to hunt the ice floes and edge at the sea. Cree had been on seal hunts with Crow on the northern ice of their homeland. Cree learned to be prepared for weather conditions on ice. The hunters would need larger more powerful bows, stronger arrows, and larger arrowheads. Heavier spears were needed for penetrating the thick skin and blubber. Crow told tales of his seal hunts when he was young. His father and other hunters told of finding ice bears far out on the ice floes. Some ice bears stood taller on hind legs than two hunters. Their fur being thick and so white the bear is almost impossible to see, blending with snow and ice. The ice bear is constantly on the hunt for seal or walrus. Ice bears are the dominant predator of the frozen north; should wolves or panthers wander too far out, they too would be prey of the ice bear. Stories were told of careless hunters being taken by the bears, leaving nothing behind other than the wooden and stone weapons of the hunter.

Cree was taking Coman on his first hunt on ice floes. They needed to pack and carry only their needs. Fire starter, bows, spears, arrows, animal hides for shelters and the heaviest of the footwear and coverings. Packed and ready they would leave the next morning.

Crow had hidden all of his fear of the danger Cree and Coman faced on the ice—fierce storms with gale-force winds blowing snow, hunters becoming separated, lost on the ice, and the menace of aggressive ice bear attack. Just as deadly was stepping onto unstable ice floe or cracks and plunging into the freezing waters of the sea. Crow worried for Coman, an exceptionally brave hunter, maybe more brave than cautious at times.

After being wished a successful hunt by Crow, the two left in search of seal on ice. Cree had also packed away knives of sharpened bone and stone as cutting and scrapping tools for skinning. He also had frozen animal fat and dry straw for starting a fire. All they packed was rolled into hide, tied on each end and strapped with rawhide across their backs.

As broken ice floes were pushed together by the ebb and flow of the sea, large broken ice chunks were pushed to the surface at the seams. Navigating these large blocks of ice made crossing the ice floes difficult and dangerous. The surface of the sea ice could not be depended on as always smooth sheets, more often being jagged and irregular. At the junction of ice floes, some drifted apart, making walking more difficult. There was the threat of hunters being on ice sheets that break, separating behind with hunters finding themselves set adrift at sea. During all times, the hunters needed to stay alert of the dangers of ice bear attack. Yes, the hazards of hunting seals were great.

The first day out was spent moving across the ice floes. Strong winds were from the direction they were traveling. Crossing ice floes used most of the daylight hours. It had become time to stop, rest, build a fire and shelter. They would stop near an ice floe seam to begin building a shelter. The two hunters took sections of broken ice, stacking one upon another as in building a wall. They built two sides with a third connecting the two. The end would be a partial opening to allow their access. The entire structure was such a height allowing enough space for sitting and building a small fire using seal fat oil. Animal skins secured by blocks of ice were placed over the entire shelter as a top.

Once inside the hunters used shavings of seal fat, dry grass, and flint to start the small fire. They placed seal fat in a stone bowl to melt and burn as heating oil. The cozy shelter with fire provided heat for warmth and for brewing a hot drink of dried berries. Enjoying the fire, the two ate dried, smoked fish and warmed themselves. The next day's trek began to a bright, cloudless blue sky. Ice crunched coldly under their footsteps as they walked on. The air was fresh, clean, and carried the smell of the sea. The two hunters were coming nearer the edge of ice and sea. Hearing the distant barks and cries of seals, they walked slowly and crouched to lower their profile. Female seals and young pups normally will be on alert for danger, remaining close to the sea edge for quick escape. Seeing the seals in the distance, Cree and Coman pulled seal skins over themselves, dropping to hands and knees. With spears in hand, they crept near to the seals, hopefully disguised well, they could move closer without alerting the seals. Once within range, the hunters would pick one seal as the target of their spears. When the target seal was struck, the others took to the sea barking and yelping alarms. Standing, they saw their target lying motionless, struck by two spears. Standing and smiling, the two walked to the seal.

Coman rolled the seal over and with a sharped-edge knife began to skin the animal. Cree, using his razor-sharp bone knife, cut open the dead animal, then removed the heart and liver to be shared later as a hunter's celebration. After emptying out the internal organs into a pile, the smell of fresh-killed seal drifted for miles.

CHAPTER FOUR
Ice Bear

The lumbering ice bear always kept his nose to the wind to catch the scent of his next meal. Ice bears had evolved over ages, prepared by nature to survive as the ruler of this unforgiving land of ice. Having huge paws with pads suitable for walking easily on ice; thick fur of hollow, insulated hair covering thick, water and windproof skin. Under this warmth of fur and skin was a five-inch layer of more insulating fat. Buoyant by thick hollow hair follicles with four large paws, made this bear a powerful and confident swimmer. Not hesitating, taking to water when stalking, it would move from floe to floe, closer and unseen by prey. The ice bear was the ultimate carnivore, perfect for stalking in the land of ice. Constantly hunting, whether on land or in water, ice bears were almost invisible in this white world of ice. The bear's clear hair coloring blended him into the background of ice and blowing snow.

Turning and lifting his nose higher into the wind, he got the scent of distant seal blood. Changing direction, the huge animal moved with determined purpose towards the two hunters and their seal.

Neither hunter had ever seen ice bears. Crouched over the seal, Coman was finishing his skinning. Looking towards the south, Coman thought he saw three black dots on the far horizon. Coman continued his skinning; the dark dots presented no danger, could be seal or walrus. Too far distant to be concerned, he convinced himself. Moving in silence to the final stage of his stalk, the ice bear had crouched down to his lowest profile, being only moments from the hunter. Now still crouched and moving ever so quickly, he was facing Coman. Looking up, Coman saw the three dark dots were much larger and not on the horizon. They were the dark eyes and nose of a huge ice bear rushing towards him.

One swinging paw and claws of the charging bear struck Coman's head, throwing him backwards. Cree, with his back towards Coman, never saw the charging bear. The force of the blow pushed Coman into the back of the standing Cree, sending him off the ice edge into the sea water. The bear dropped on Coman, and with one quick bite to his neck, it was over. Spinning around the hungry bear began to feed on the seal.

Cree with heavy, chilling, water-soaked clothing pulling him down, clung to the ice edge by his bare fingers. With only head and hands above water, too heavily soaked to pull up. He would climb out only to face the hungry bear. If not, he would freeze in the water. Cree wondered how he could survive this. Thinking, what would Crow do?

Reaching down in the water, feeling for his knife, he pulled it from its sheath. Holding to the ice with one hand, the knife in the other raised high, he drove its point down into the ice. Chipping ice out again, and again until Cree had a hollowed-out hand grip. Holding his knife, he drove it into the hollowed-out ice. It held firm, giving him leverage to pull up to his shoulders. Holding tightly to the knife with his other, he reached on the ice, feeling for his spear. Gripping it by the wooden shaft he pulled it towards himself and gripped it closely to the stone spearhead. With a firm grip, he began chipping and hollowing out ice.

Being heavier and having more bulk, the spearhead quickly chipped away and dug a hole into the ice. Gripping the hole with his hand and dug in knife in the other, he pulled himself up high enough to get one leg up onto the ice, then rolled over, pulling and freeing himself from the water. Cree saw his brother Coman had been killed by the attack. Not seeing the bear near, there was a bloody trail of seal being dragged away by the bear to finish his feast later. The skinned hide of the seal was left behind, still having a layer of fat on the underside. Cree began to quickly remove all of Coman's dry clothing, leggings, and footwear.

At the same time, he pulled off his own wet clothing and put on the dry. Coman carried fire starter in a leather pouch strapped over his head and shoulder. Cree opened the pouch, taking dry grass, a block of animal fat, flint, and mineral stone. Arranging the seal skin in a heap and dry grass and shaving from the block of dried fat, he struck flint until sparks ignited the grass to smoldering. Holding and blowing, the grass and dried fat soon had the seal skin fat and hide flaming. Setting down by the warm fire, Cree rested and mourned his brother. Cree knew flying scavengers or the bear would come for Coman, so he took his brother's spear, knife, and headwear and slid Coman over the ice edge into the sea, watching him sink until out of sight. Now dry and warm, he gathered his things, turned with the wind to his back and began at a trot towards his waiting family camp.

CHAPTER FIVE

Southward from the Land Bridge

Crow could wait no longer for his two sons. He, Koda, and Pawee must follow the caribou and seek a land with forest. Forest provided fuel for fire, and cover for shelter. The animals they follow would be seeking more grasslands. Elk and bison had a preference for browsing and the cover of forest. Forest provided the thickness of brushy forest giving shelter from artic winds and cover from rain and snow. Forest also provided more protection from the larger predators, which preferred to hunt the grassland.

After crossing the Beringia land bridge, Crow led his small group southward still in search of forested land. Crow had taught Cree since boyhood skills needed to survive as a hunter. As Cree grew in knowledge and age, Crow had given him more leadership over their family. Coman, being younger, followed closely to Cree's lead. Hunting, crafting tools, teaching Koda, they were together as one. Crow was a rugged muscular man with long hair, some facial hair, and wearing clothing and footwear of hides and fur of animals he had hunted. Always with bow and arrow that he had crafted, his clothing and footwear were of Pawee's craftmanship. Crow now would lead their path until his sons returned. Little did Crow know how historic his family's journey across the land bridge would be. Their journey would lead the way to great lands for human people to live.

No sign of any other people now or before had they found. Perhaps in past centuries, ancient people had entered this gateway to a new world. The great ice age had covered this land farther than any eagle could fly. People and animals of the past would have faced a stark land of ice. People would have also faced overwhelming odds against survival.

As they moved farther south, Crow saw many herds of grazing animals across the land. In the distant east was a great range of majestic mountains. With peaks covered in snow, Crow, Koda, and Pawee were in awe of the beauty of this land. The forests, skies, rivers, the air they breathed was fresh and clean. They could smell the fragrance of the distant forest of pine and evergreens. The herds of animals, the fragrance of the land, mountains, streams, and blue sky all of one common thread. Undisturbed wildlife and land.

Seeing the mountains brought back thoughts to Pawee stories told by her mother. Tales her mother was told by her grandmother when she lived in a faraway land. A tribe of savage people who would raid smaller tribes or groups taking young women and children captive, disappearing into the forest, to be never seen again by their families. They were known as the painted or marked people of the highlands. Their men had no hair on their face or head, but had drawn symbols and lines painted in white on their bodies and face. Painted people would raid with bows, clubs, hatchets, killing, and taking captives. The young Pawee and her sisters were told these tales to keep them close to camp. If raids ever came, they were to run to the forest and hide.

Pawee had been born into her family, which was of a distant land from Crow's family. Pawee's father and his group of hunters would sometimes join Crow's in hunting large herds of bison or mammoth. As Pawee grew older, her father decided she would join Crow's group to become the heart mate (wife) of Cree. Crow happily agreed and welcomed Pawee into their family. There was a celebration feast of bison meat and drink around a campfire as well as gifts of bow and arrows from Crow to Pawee's father. Pawee also received boots and a necklace crafted by her sisters as gifts from her family.

As they went farther to the south, the more forest they found. Crow and Koda continued to hunt elk or caribou for meat. Keme the wolf, raised from a pup, stayed close to Crow other than on hunts. Hunting with Crow would not be good for Keme's wolf scent would put the hunted game animal on alert of danger. Being wolf, Keme's natural instincts to pursue and kill are strong, so hunting with Crow would be difficult for Keme to contain. When Crow was on hunts, Keme normally stayed close to Pawee in camp. In the event of danger, Keme would be sure to sound alarm and come to protect Pawee.

CHAPTER SIX
Wolves

Sixteen-year-old Koda was also a brave hunter, much the same as Cree and Crow. He was muscular, stood taller than Cree or Crow, had long dark hair, and intense dark eyes. Koda watched Crow and learned the craft of making bows, arrows, and shafts for hunting large and small animals. He learned how to shape and sharpen flint, shale rock, and large animal bone into spearheads, arrowheads, and knives. He learned making tools and techniques for fishing with spear, arrows, or building and trapping fish in shallow water.

Koda carried bow, arrows, and a slender shaft spear with a spearhead made of sharpened bone to a nearby stream for fishing. The stream had fast-running clear water, a smooth rocky bottom, and rocky banks. Standing quietly in shallow water with spear raised at ready, waiting for any fish to swim close, Koda successfully speared two fish, tossing them on the stream bank. One more and he would have enough for tonight's meal. Looking upstream, Koda saw an elk cow and her calf bolt in panic as they crossed upstream. Koda froze in place, daring not draw attention to himself. He knew the elk were fleeing in fear. They were being chased.

Remaining motionless, he watched as two wolves ran across the stream focused on the fleeing elk. Before Koda could step out and take cover in nearby brush, he looked upstream and out stepped a third wolf. Stopping midstream, turning, and looking directly toward Koda. Knowing there was high-water erosion along the upper bank, Koda rushed to a washout that had a rock overhang. Being large enough for him to crawl into, he pushed his back against the rear wall. Seeing the wolf running across the stream and coming towards him, Koda pushed back even more but not before the snarling wolf grabbed him by his leggings.

Taking his fishing spear, he jabbed the wolf's nose. The small fishing spear was not strong enough to inflict real injury, but with a narrow sharp point, it drove the wolf back, causing it to release its grip. Digging his heels into the dirt, Koda pushed himself back into the washout as far as possible, but still the snapping wolf came back again and again. Taking his knife in hand, he slashed at the wolf each time it came after his legs. There was no holding off the large wolf, it had driven Koda as deep back as he could go.

Koda gripped his knife in one hand, then raised and bent the other arm across his face and neck to protect himself. Then, leaning forward and closer to the wolf, it grabbed the bent arm. With his free arm, Koda drove his knife deep into the wolf's neck; again and again he stabbed the wolf's neck. Gushing blood, the wounded wolf fell back, stumbled, and dropped. The wolf lay and took its last breath.

Koda had never felt anger towards a wild animal. When this wolf came after him, grabbed his leg and then his arm, he felt hate. Who was this wolf to attack and think to kill him? Koda thought, *I am a hunter, a brave hunter.* Perhaps a pack or all three wolves would attack, but not a lone wolf. Walking out and kneeling beside the wolf, he took his knife, cut off the head and skinned the wolf. With adrenaline still flowing, Koda had his first kill of a deadly predator. The wolf head would be a trophy of his manhood and power as a hunter. Taking his trophy and stopping to pick up his fish, he proudly headed back to camp.

Pawee looked up seeing Koda walking to camp. She got an excited smile recognizing the trophy he was carrying. She was proud for her strong son. Keme the wolf went running out, tail wagging, to greet Koda. Pawee hugged Koda, letting him know she was pleased. She was thinking *he is much like his father, a brave hunter*. She saw the sleeve of his coat and leggings were torn and ripped. He must have fought off a wolf attack. Crow also was glad for Koda, patting him on the shoulder to show his approval, Crow was thinking *Koda is coming into a true hunter.* After Koda tossed the wolf head and skin to the ground, Keme went over to the head and took a sniff. Keme had not seen another wolf since being a weeks-old pup. Sniffing, Keme recognized the scent as one of his kind. Turning and trotting back to Pawee, he gave her a tail wag and tongue lick on her hand.

CHAPTER SEVEN
Following Sign

Cree had traveled the ice floes for two days before finally reaching solid land. Having not eaten for three days Cree began hunting small game, rabbits, rodents, whatever he could find to eat. He needed to find the direction to his last camp. Hopefully his family would still be there. If not, he was sure they would be following the caribou migrating to grasslands in the south. When traveling, their typical camp would be brushy shrubs with animal-hide covering for shelter. Quick to build and quick to roll up and move on—that would be Crow's choice. Walking up, he recognized the campsite along with the remains of their last fire. Cree knew Crow would leave sign of the direction they were traveling. Circling, he found four stones arraigned in a straight line with three larger stones across the top that indicated their traveling direction.

Cree stopped to hunt, build a fire, eat, and rest before leaving to follow Crow's sign.

Cree took caution when following the herd animals. He watched from cover as two lions stalked a group of bison. The cave lions stood five feet at the shoulders, were tail to nose 10′ and weighing up to 700 pounds. These massive lions were the ancestors of the smaller lions that later roamed prehistoric America. The two cave lions attacked and easily pulled down a mature bull bison. Staying hidden, Cree waited for the lions to have their fill and leave the area.

After leaving their kill, Cree approached and cut meat from the carcass for himself. He quickly returned to the cover of the tree line. Wolves or bear were apt to pick up the scent of the bison remains. After eating, Cree continued cautiously traveling to the south. Being a fearless hunter, Cree was well taught by Crow. In the past Cree, Coman, and Crow together had fought off large predators, but alone, Cree stood little chance and would remain wary of his surroundings.

Going on, Cree found more sign left by Crow—a stone marker indicating their direction. Stooped down and his back towards the forest tree line, Cree suddenly felt uneasy, sensing he was being watched. Standing, he turned to the forest but saw nothing, only motionless trees. Seeing nothing, he relied on his senses. He was being watched. There were always dangers in the forest, so he would stay alert. Stepping forward, he moved on southward, following his family.

Deeper in the forest, standing hidden in the trees, it was watching Cree. It had quietly been following and watching him. Moving silently back into the forest, it remained unseen as Cree walked away.

CHAPTER EIGHT
Pawee and Hidden Shelter

Pawee was a slender woman with black hair that went beyond her shoulders. With dark eyes and always a pleasant smile, she was a problem-solving worker who pleased herself by caring well for her family.

Light snow was beginning to fall; it was now time to continue south. Pawee had crafted a small sled of animal hide held in shape by strong shaped tree branches. Pawee had made strapping from long strips of fiber from evergreens and animal sinew. She removed bark from live trees, then peeled the exposed fiber from the tree. Taking two or three strips of fiber, she wound and twisted it into strapping for holding the sled together. With thick tough bison hide as the bottom, it was strong and sturdy. Loaded with animal furs, skins, extra footwear, and clothing, the bison-hide-bottom sled could easily be pulled over the snow and ice.

Members of Pawee's homeland people had herded reindeer in Siberia. During Siberian winter, hunting animals for food was difficult and required hunters to travel in harsh conditions for long distances to find game animals. The Siberian dark season climate was extreme, making game animal population few. They also traveled constantly, searching for browse, twigs, or moss. Reindeer were used to pull sleds or pack animals for the long hunting trips. Reindeer could survive the harshest of conditions and from being herded were easier to work as a domesticated animal. Pawee and Cree acquired two reindeer as a gift when they became heart mates. They were larger males and easily pulled a sled or carried a pack. Normally one pulled the sled and the other carried the pack.

Pawee hand made many items used by Crow and Koda for hunting and fishing. Pawee was quite good at fishing and using a bow and arrow. She fashioned snowshoes from rawhide and birch branch, fishing line from plant fiber, and fish hooks from small bone. In addition to fishing, she was a good small-game hunter and made most of the clothing.

After eating fish for their last meal of the day, Crow announced they would pack up camp and continue on tomorrow morning. Crow thought to himself how much safer their travel would be with Cree and Coman with them. Crow had left sign there showing their travel direction. To himself Crow thought, *if alive they should have already been with us.* Crow kept their fire burning during the night.

With the snow still falling the next morning, Pawee and Koda loaded the sled, attaching to the reindeer with a harness of rawhide. The other reindeer Koda packed with more hides, parts of the shelter frame, and coverings. With Crow and Keme leading the way, Koda and Pawee followed with reindeer and sled. As they moved farther south, Crow thought with the season changing to green, the streams and rivers were thawing, the forest coming back to green, and they would not need to push themselves as hard. After traveling a few days, they could rest, camp, hunt meat, and continue to cross the great mountain range before cold and snow season began again.

If they could cross the mountains and find a land where they could hunt, fish, gather nuts and berries during most seasons, they would look for other groups of hunters. Crow also knew some day Koda will go farther and find his own territory and family. For now, Crow decided they should stop and camp before nightfall. It was still snowing; they needed to build shelter and a fire. Crow found a suitable site along the wood line with brush and thick evergreens. Crow took animal skins tied to brush and tied to limbs for cover. He then took more skins and staked them to the ground and tied to more limbs to block wind and blowing snow.

Pawee and Koda looked for firewood. Going deeper into the woods, Koda used a precaution method taught by his father, Cree. Taking his knife, he scaled off the bark down to the fiber of trees, doing this on the opposite side from camp of the tree. He also would take short young trees and bend to the direction of camp. When returning in late light, he could find his way back. As he was picking up wood and placing it on their sled, Pawee called to him. She was bent down and moving through some thick brush partially covered with thick evergreen branches. She thought perhaps hunters had built this during extreme weather.

Koda thought differently. It looked more like a covered, well put together and hidden nest or resting place. Without any sign of a campfire site, having a very strong odor, it surely was a bedding place of a large animal. Koda told Pawee they should gather their firewood and move back to camp. Leading the reindeer pulling the heavily loaded sled, Koda thought how strange evergreen limbs being placed as cover over the shelter by an animal. Maybe a bear could do this? Or would for hibernation? This is a new land, could be a strange animal unknown to Koda.

Much later that night, it stood in the darkness watching the three sitting by a campfire. What were these creatures? Dropping back into deep woods, it knew blowing wind and falling snow would cover any tracks left behind.

The next morning Pawee placed a hollowed stone bowl filled with water over the coals of the fire. She then took dried berries from last season, crushed them in her hand, and dropped them into the bowl of boiling water to give flavor for a hot drink that she poured into three wooden cups. That and some fresh fire-cooked rabbit meat would give a boost for today's journey. Keme was fed well with any food not eaten or that hunters brought back to camp. He especially enjoyed bison and bison bone. Keme also stayed on alert for any squirrel or rabbit that strayed too close. The reindeer were self-sufficient, browsing on grass, twigs, or leaves.

The snowfall had stopped during the night, leaving a bright blue sky and the warmth of the sun to enjoy. Looking up, Crow saw ducks and geese flying to the north while elk and bison were coming out of the forest to warm in the sun—green season was coming.

Walking on, Crow saw how much closer were the mountains. Once there they would make camp, hunt, fish, rest, and wait for the warmth of the green season. Then they could trek around the mountains. Koda was looking forward to the complete thawing of rivers and streams, the good fishing and hunting. The taste and energy from eating fresh meat and fish flamed over a hot fire was to look forward to. For fishing, Pawee would weave fish traps of limbs and hemp. She would also make snare traps for Koda and Crow's rabbit hunting. They were preparing themselves for crossing the mountain pass and valleys.

Crow continued leaving sign for his sons Cree and Coman to follow.

CHAPTER NINE
Cree finds Smoke

For Cree, fishing was almost impossible. Unless you could find a lake or stream with thin or broken ice, fish may not be found. His diet was now rabbit or occasional found seeds or nuts. To keep moving and following sign left behind by Crow, Cree did not stop to rest or hunt other than to a build fire for warmth or cooking meat. Cree longed to be with his family. He wanted to hunt with Crow and Koda, to fish with Pawee. Cree wanted to be there to protect them from any danger.

Cree thought about his brother, Coman, how they talked about traveling to new lands of warmth and green. Land of abundant animals to hunt. Plentiful in food of plants, nuts, berries. His family's previous land was cold, and lacked an abundance of food sources. Cree's group had been larger, yet came to share their territory with two other tribes. Their land could not support all of the families and groups, there was not enough to feed all. That led to fighting between the groups leading to Crow and Cree's decision to seek new land.

Cree knew to be wary and avoid other groups. When younger he had been told stories by Crow of bands of people with painted markings covering their faces, arms, and hands. They had no hair on the head. It also was marked with white paint. They carried spears and long knives for killing, not hunting. They would attack other groups, taking whatever they wanted.

When Cree and Coman were young boys, their group's hunting party led by Crow had gone to a distant hunting ground for bison. Many days later when the hunters returned, all shared a meal of fresh bison. After darkness, Crow sat everyone around the fire and told a story of finding a lone woman wandering in the forest. The woman was ragged, dirty clothes, had scratches, bruises, was cold and hungry. The hunters built a fire to warm and dry her clothes. They gave the woman dried meat and water. She told the hunters how her tribe had been attacked by the painted people, killing some of her men, taking her and a young girl with them. She told how they traveled for four days through the forest with little food or rest before getting to their camp.

This woman told how the camp was ill kept, decorated with skulls and bones. Rotting never-cured animal hides, animal heads, animal antlers, tusks, and horns were scattered about their camp. She told Crow of their women being poorly treated and clothed. They spoke in a language she did not understand. After a few days, some men left camp, going on a hunt and taking the young girl with them. The woman never saw the girl again. The men and women in camp would eat raw meat. They drank a heated brew that was foul to taste. Some of the captives were kept as workers.

They were to gather firewood and keep fires burning, provide meals, gather food, and repair clothing. And it came to pass, the woman gained the trust of her captors. Late in the day before darkness, she was instructed to gather wood for the night's fire. Pulling along a basket for wood, she gathered and returned firewood to camp. Telling there was more to be gotten, she returned leaving the basket. Once in the forest, she began to walk quickly for a distance, then she ran, then running as fast as a forest would allow. Away from her captors she ran as never before.

When darkness came, she stayed running until the distance was safe. Finding a thick tree, she climbed high, away from any followers or wild beast's sight. She took the tether used to pull the firewood basket and tied herself to the tree so as not to fall when asleep. The forest was loud of distant howling beast. Hearing no captors' footsteps or voices, she slept. There was great danger to any and all who walked the forest in the night.

She told of walking the days into darkness without rest. At dark she slept in the trees for safety. She ate any insects or dead animal she came across. The woman had been lost in the forest for many days, knowing she had been traveling north when captured, south is where her safety would be found. Asking the woman of looking for her family or staying with the hunters, the woman wanted to continue south. Crow and his hunters made her a spear with sharpened spearhead for hunting and protection. Leaving her with some food, the hunters continued east.

Remembering tales of vicious painted people gave Cree reason when finding sign left by Crow to scatter so any others would not recognize and follow. Cree had not seen any tracks in snow other than those of animals. Having seen no fire or smoke, Cree felt he and his family were alone in this land.

Cree thought about Pawee, how she had been his companion since a young girl. She had been taught well by her mother and people of her tribe. She scraped, stretched, and dried animal skins for Cree and Crow. She knew the art of scraping limbs into arrow or spear shafts. Pawee made cooking tools, handles for stone or flint cutting tools as axe or pounding like a club. She was a relevant member of the family. Pawee would make bow string for Cree, Crow, and Koda from animal muscle sinew. She would take leg tendons from the larger animals for its elasticity. When stretched and two twisted together, it became extremely strong for a most powerful bow pull. Cree had lost his bow and arrows during the ice bear attack, dropping it into the water. Not having the bow made his hunting small game for food more difficult.

In the far distance looking past the forest, Cree saw clouds of thick gray smoke rising above the trees. Hopefully this was his family and not some unknowns. Gathering his things, he was quickly on his way.

CHAPTER TEN
Strange Tracks

Crow, Pawee, and Koda gathered fallen and broken dead tree branches, limbs, and brush for most of the morning. Stacking them on the sled, they needed both reindeer to pull. Getting another load and another. All was placed into a large pile at the edge of the forest. It was a tremendous pile and would make a great fire. If Cree and Coman were following, they would see this smoke from a great distance. Taking hot coal from their campfire and placing it in the pile of brush, it grew through the brush, dry limbs, into the logs to a great fire. When the fire was at a height and burning hot, they then began throwing fresh evergreen foliage onto the fire. As they did, the evergreens burned and created great billows of smoke rising high above the forest.

Koda with bow and arrows went hunting rabbit or maybe even better fat little ground hens. Everyone ate ground hens—what a treat. They could fly and roosted low in trees, yet spent most of their time on the ground or in thick brush, looking for insects, grubs, and berries. They were a wary fowl, ran fast, and were not easy to shoot with bow and arrow. Pawee could cook in the campfire, adding some plants or roots.

As Koda walked through the forest, he heard the calling of high-flying geese. *What a sight*, he thought to himself. Countless honking geese flying in smaller groups, each group in uniform formation following a single lead goose on lead point. One leader to find their path to distant and ancient nesting grounds. Waterfowl had flown these skies for ages, seeking their yearly nesting grounds to raise young before flying back south ahead of the change of seasons to ice and snow.

Koda knew the signs of clear and sun-warmed skies were the coming of the green season—a time when the animals would give birth to their young and eggs would be in nests, colored berries, flowers blooming, growing vines and plants, finding plants and underground roots and bulbs for food. Some Pawee will make into drink or nourishment. Green season brings good hunting; Koda remembered the teachings of Crow and Cree. When hunting in green season, leave the young, take the old. When taking eggs from a nest, leave more than you take. Never take the young from the nest and never kill the mother elk or bison when they have a suckling. The young, when left to grow, will eventually give back more to the hunter than he has taken. Crow taught if we are of care with nature, she will provide and care for us.

There continued to be snow covering the ground in and out of the forest, especially in the shaded areas. Walking deeper into the woods, Koda came to a running stream that had begun to thaw and the ice break. Pleasantly he was thinking of soon he would be fishing. Crossing the stream, he came upon some tracks in the snow that he didn't recognize. Several tracks were large and odd in shape, perhaps a bear. At that moment he saw movement over his shoulder. Slowly turning and pulling an arrow back in the bowstring, he released, striking a plump ground hen. Smiling, he picked up his prize hen and headed back to camp, no longer thinking of the strange tracks he had found.

Back in camp, Crow made known they should pack and move on toward the mountains. He told Pawee and Koda the fire smoke had been great enough to be seen from far away. If seen by Cree and Coman, they would for certain know which direction to travel. Pawee had made some changes to the sled, adding thin strips of wood for each bottom side to act as runners over grass and snow. With the reindeer pulling, the sled would move more easily over most ground.

After some days of travel, the three reached the foothills of the mountain range. Following the herds that were seeking long-ago trails to grazing land, Crow was pleased. They had found vast forested land cut through the mountains by prehistoric bygone glaciers. It was an enormous green land. A paradise of grazing bison, elk, and caribou. There was tundra and marshland for tens of thousands of waterfowl, forest of assorted mixtures of trees, with rivers and streams full of fish. This was a land Crow had wished to find for his family. In this landscape, nature provides water, shelter, and food for waterfowl, birds, grazing animals, and animals of the forest.

Since leaving their homeland of eastern Siberia, this was the dream Crow sought.

CHAPTER ELEVEN
Cree's Homecoming

Koda picked up his bow and arrows as he stared to the north. Taking a few steps forward, he notched an arrow. Crow, watching, stood and asked what was happening. Standing with Keme the wolf beside Koda, he, too, could see a dark figure moving in the distance. Asking Pawee for his bow and arrows. Crow crouched down and motioned Koda and Pawee do the same. The figure was moving near a tree line to hide its silhouette. As it came closer, they could see it was a man, a hunter in tattered clothing. Walking, carrying a spear and having a bundle strapped to his back. Standing up together they could see it was Cree. It was really Cree. At last! Pawee and Koda could not hold their excitement. They hugged one another. But he was alone. Where is Coman?

After shared embraces and greetings, Cree sat by the fire and asked for water. Pawee quickly brought him drink. Cree was exhausted, hungry, his clothes were torn. Pawee brought bison for him to eat. Sitting around the fire, Crow asked Cree, "Where is Coman?" Cree told the story of their seal hunt, about the attack by ice bear, praising his brother, Coman, as being a mighty hunter. Cree told of his being in the water, how he escaped the water getting back on ice, being so cold, and building a fire. Cree told of spending the night on ice floes, of he and Coman building an ice shelter.

Koda listened closely, wanting to hear every detail of Cree's journey. Cree told of hunting rabbit, of spending some nights up in trees if wolves were heard close. Koda very much listened to the story of the two lions taking down bison. Cree told of staying close to tree lines to better avoid predators. Pawee was as taken with Cree's storytelling as Koda. Keme sat between them with his head on Pawee's lap. Occasionally, he wagged his tail, asking for a pat on the head. Cree explained about scattering the sign of direction so as not to be followed. The smoke from their huge fire rose so high above the forest it was easily seen. He wanted family to know he never gave up hope of finding them. Pawee fed all dried caribou meat and hot drink of berries. Crow announced tomorrow they would hunt fresh meat for a celebration feast honoring the safe return of Cree. The three went to sleep thinking of Coman, and his greatness as a hunter.

The next morning as the hunters were preparing to leave, Pawee presented to Cree a flat bundle neatly wrapped in deer skin. Inside was a newly made bow, arrows, with a quiver made of leather and fur. Cree was pleased. He saw this bow was powerful for larger game with arrows of sharpened flint.

Walking through thick forest, Koda was in the middle with Crow to one side and Cree the other. Spread apart at a distance, unseen by the others. Hearing the thrashing of running deer, soon after a whistling call signal from Crow. He had arrowed a deer. Catching up with Koda, Cree and he followed to Crow's whistle. At a small clearing in the forest, Cree and Koda came to a stop. In front of them were three large boulders stacked one on another. The three stacked higher than one man. The boulders had been there for ages. Moss had grown on the north side. No markings nor human tracks.

Cree gave three quick whistle calls to Crow. They had hunted deep into the forest, going a very long distance. When Crow came, seeing the three boulders, he quietly put one finger to his lips for silence and motioned to follow him out of the forest. They walked for a while, not speaking, being as quiet as possible. As they neared out of the forest, Crow explained they should now continue their hunt for meat for celebration tonight.

As they began, Koda asked Crow about the boulders, the deer, the silence, before he could finish, Crow said, "Later." They found elk but let them pass; elk would be too much meat for tonight. Finally, spotting deer moving out of a thicket, Cree shot with his arrow. They skinned and took deer meat they needed, leaving the rest for scavengers and wolves or bear. The hunter took only what they needed, not wanting to waste. Walking into camp, Pawee had a fire waiting for the hunters.

They had a meal of charred deer roast done in hot coal with plant roots, wild beets, and onion. They were joyful to have Cree back with them. Pawee was pleased knowing he had killed his first game with her gift bow. Afterward,

Pawee presented all three hunters with a special treat. A thick, dried, hard woody vine grown along trees. The vine was hollow with thickness of a finger. Broken into lengths of a finger it could be lit with flame from a fire and smoked. When smoked, the vine had a sweet taste and aroma. The three sat, smoking and staring at the moon and flickering stars. Cree's thoughts were of Koda and how he was growing into a man.

After finishing the meal and smoking, Koda again asked about the three boulders in the forest. Asked why they left the killed deer behind. All four sat in darkness around the fire as Crow began by repeating the story of the people with drawings on their faces, heads, arms, and legs. About their being savages, being disrespectful of the spirits of the animals of the forest, and being killers of humans. They were territorial of their own land, yet would cross into others territory to take that land. They would kill animals for only the horns or hides, not always for the meat as food. These people did not respect the wilderness, taking all they could and leaving nothing behind.

Crow then began to tell a story he had never told them. A story told when Crow was a very young boy. A story told to Crow's father's father when he was young—a story of ancient hunters in an ancient land, far away from their homeland, an ancient land of thick deep forest, forest that grew at the base of the greatest mountains of all. So high their peaks reached up through the clouds, staying snow covered through the changing seasons. So great were the mountains no hunter could climb to the peak or cross to the other side. Ancient hunters had climbed the mountains only to disappear in the clouds never to be seen again. As high as all the mountains were, one was the most majestic. So high it looked down on the others. So high the story is told the most powerful of soaring eagles could not reach its peak. The most ancient people called this mountain "Father of all Mountains."

These great frozen mountains and high elevations were the home to many animals. Crow continued his storytelling of the many mountain animals that lived and survived on the rocky cliffs and ice. Animals sure-footed with long-hair shaggy coats of thick fur. Leopards that lived in the cold of the heights and as sure-footed as their prey. Wolves that lived and hunted as individuals and not in packs, prowled the lover levels, hunting for the weak and young. Long-haired bears that hunted the upper forest and mountains. These mountain bears were continually moving, searching for prey. The forest surrounding the base of the mountains was home to saber-tooth tiger, mastodon, wooly rhinoceros, oxen, fox, and small game.

As Crow continued telling this story of ancient times, Koda's thoughts were drifting to *what does this have to do with today's three boulders?* Crow then, looking at Cree and Koda, told of the most ancient of the mountain inhabitants. The first who came to live in those forest, and mountains. Crow's people had passed these tales down through the ages. Those ancient creatures of the mountains came to be known as the "Others."

The Others of the mountains were of great size. Some as tall as two humans. The Others were of long arms and tall legs. Powerful with large muscular bodies and broad shoulders. Large hands, muscular arms and legs. Having large faces with powerful mouths and teeth, their bodies were covered in thick furry coats of hair. Only the face and palm of hands were not covered in hair. The face and palms were of a thick leathery skin that was very rugged and protective. Others had no language, spoke no words. Others communicated with whistling, howls, yelps, cries, and warning growls. Others had no fire, or knowledge to create fire, only a fear of fire. Others had no tools, spears, clubs, or any weapons. When living in the mountains, Others make bedding nests in caves, in the forest sheltering in brushy cover. Others ate much the same foods as humans. Only killing animals for the meat they needed.

It was told Others could run down the fastest deer, move through the forest in silence, take down large prey using their powerful strength. The large males were feared by the most fiercest beast. Bears, panther, and humans avoided the territory of Others. Others honored and respected nature and the animals of the wilderness. They respected what the Father of Mountains provided, eating meat, nuts, berries, plants, roots, all gifts of nature. Crow explained the Others are the protectors of the wilderness, "as we hunters are to be." Others also use sign to message with humans.

The three boulders were sign. Placed there by Others. "They left sign giving us a message to not pass the boulders. Those were their forests of Others and their wildlife." Finishing his story with himself had never seen the creatures or their sign until today. The Others live in the mountains or deep in the darkest forest. According to Crow, we were never to go back to the Three Boulders.

CHAPTER TWELVE

Creatures

The next day Koda would go hunting for elk, deer, or caribou. They needed meat and hides for clothing or shelter cover. Koda also wanted to prove he could be the brave hunter that Coman had been. Koda wished to now be included on the long or dangerous hunts with Cree and Crow. He wanted to show Cree and Crow through his actions he was now a brave hunter. Koda did not realize he was already thought of as such and need not any more to prove himself. Their typical life before had been hunting daily for their needs. After beginning this journey for a new land, they had not had the opportunity to hunt daily.

With bow, knife, and spear, Koda began early back into the forest. Going deep into the woods, he knew he would be close to the boundary stones. He decided they had been there for ages, and if creatures had lived in that forest, it was probably in ancient times. While hunting, Koda saw through the trees a large bull elk with great antlers. The elk was moving across in front of Koda. With bow and arrow at ready, he positioned himself behind a large tree. With its head down, it browsed as it walked a path crossing directly in front of Koda. The elk was at a short distance, and taking aim, Koda stepped out and released an arrow, striking the elk behind the left front shoulder.

Reacting to being struck by an arrow the bull leaped, and ran in a burst of energy through the brushy undergrowth away from the direction of Koda's arrow. Remaining still and quiet, Koda listened for the sound of the heavy bull to go crashing to the ground. The elk had run far through the thick brush before the loss of blood brought him down. Hearing the bull crash to the ground,

Koda remained still, listening for the bull's final death moan. Hearing nothing more, cautiously he moved closer to the bull.

Finally standing close, he saw the bull was a massive elk with large antlers that were of great size. Having so much meat, large skin, and antlers, Cree and Crow would respect his ability as a hunter. He took his knife and began to remove the head and skin of the elk. He took the skin and rolled and tied it, placing it across and tied with sinew to the antlers. He then pulled the heavy antlers across his back. With all in place, he shifted to balance the weight. He was ready to begin the long walk to camp.

Coming very near to camp, he dropped his load to the ground, and now would go back to complete butchering the elk. He would bring the entire hind quarter to camp making a great surprise for his family. Getting back to the elk, he began removing the tenderloins and one meaty hind quarter including the leg. Later Crow and Cree will return with him to retrieve all of the elk meat.

As Koda wrapped the hind quarter in protective skin for his pulling along the forest floor he heard yelping cries of an animal running quickly through the forest. What he saw was a young bear being chased by several wolves. The young bear was fast to stay ahead of the wolves. Packs of wolves were known by hunters for their natural chase endurance. As the lead wolves would slow the followers would pull up and continue the chase. Even the most powerful or fastest of prey would eventually succumb to chasing wolves. Wolves like most hunters would kill in accordance with natural laws of the wilderness. Normally targeting the weak, the old, the injured.

The young bear was looking for a tree to escape up. Coming to a towering evergreen with thick branches it began to climb up. Two wolves grabbed the foot and leg. With yelping cries the young bear could not pull away. It seemed the young bear was more calling for help rather than the pain of wolf attack. Koda took aim with bow and arrow, hitting the foot-biting wolf. It fell with an arrow through its neck. Koda moved closer and saw this was not a young bear but rather some unknown creature. It was two-legged and ran standing on two feet. It continued the yelping cries while swinging a clinched hand at the wolf gripped to its leg. Hanging to a higher limb it could not pull free from the wolves. Koda sent a killing arrow into the second wolf tearing at the creature's leg. As that wolf fell a third attacked the creature trying to pull the creature from its grip to the tree. Wolf four turned, saw the source of the arrows, and came for Koda. Quick to aim and release, Koda's arrow flew into the fourth wolf. The remaining two wolves were gripped to the leg and foot of the yelping creature.

As Koda watched a very large dark figure tore through the brush and grabbed one wolf by the hind legs and slammed it into a tree, killing the wolf. Grabbing the last wolf still holding to the young creature, the large creature snapped its neck, killing the last wolf. The large creature reached up and gently helped the smaller one from the tree and sat it on the ground. Looking around, the larger saw three more wolves around the tree killed by arrows. Turning and seeing the frozen-in-place Koda, the large creature, showed its teeth and fangs, sending Koda a warning growl. Standing the younger creature on both legs, it was encouraged to walk away, but limping and dragging its foot, the larger picked up the young one and walked away, turning their heads once to look back at Koda.

That was the last Koda saw of the two creatures. These were the ancient creatures of the wilderness. The creatures of the Great Mountains, Crow had spoken of. The Others. Koda gathered his bow, arrows, elk meat, and headed back to camp. As he walked, he decided what he had seen was not meant for him to speak of. He would not tell anyone of what he had seen. No one would he tell. These were the protectors of the wilderness, part of keeping a balance in the circle of life. Their boundaries must be honored.

Koda returned to camp to get the reindeer and sled. Going back to where he had dropped the elk meat and skin, he loaded all and led the reindeer to camp. Not speaking of any details of the elk hunt or where he hunted. Koda quietly worked with Pawee to scrape and stretch the elk hide. After finishing, Koda gave Keme a good-size meaty elk bone he'd set aside as a special treat. Trotting off holding bone in mouth, Keme found his favorite resting place to enjoy his elk.

CHAPTER THIRTEEN
Green Season Camp

Before going any farther in their nomadic journey Cree, Crow, and Koda would begin to hunt bear and bison. The family can use more meat and fish to preserve by drying or smoking. More animal skins to replace worn clothing, footwear, and shelter coverings. Pawee stayed busy gathering fresh berries, building fish and small animal traps, and stone tools while the men were out hunting. As usual Keme would be in camp with Pawee.

The three hunters worked making new arrows and spear heads, sharpening knives, along with skinning and scraping tools. The hunters needed dependable sharp weapons; they would be facing the largest bear of that time; as large as an ice bear, the short-faced bear was also a deadly carnivore. The bears preyed on bison, young mastodon, wild horses, or any other unfortunate grazing animals that wandered too close.

The hunters packed with all their needs for a successful hunt wanted to stay within a one-day walk to camp. Taking a skid of animal skins and wooden branches they would need to pull back to camp as much meat, bone, and skin as possible. Once they found a bear, they would attack with bow and arrow from three sides. Each hunter independent of the other with all shooting arrows in unison. Once striking the bear with multiple arrows, the hunters would close in with heavy spears to finish killing the animal. If the bear charged, the hunters must stand in place and hold their spear as such for the bear charge to impale itself. Hopefully the bear would not charge but stand and defend itself for a safer kill by the hunters.

Later that day they found a male bear feeding on a bison it had killed. As planned, they formed a semicircle, being sure not to be seen by the bear. On

Cree's hand signal, each moved closer to the bear and began shooting arrows. Being surprised at being struck over and over by arrows, the bear did not know which direction to protect itself. Each hunter fired three or more arrows. Each hunter's arrows had hit their target. The bear remained crouched protectively over the bison not yet seeing his attackers. Wounded by arrows and raising its head, the bear looked forward, picked a target, and charged. With his spear in hand Crow drove the end of the spear shaft into the ground angled to the charging bear. Cree and Koda came in closer to Crow jabbing spears into the bear's side.

As it rose on its hind legs, Crow drove his spear into the lower chest of the bear. Falling to the ground, the huge bear lay, taking the last of its breath. Most large animals shot by hunter's arrow or speared will run some distance before falling to the ground. The dying animal will usually make a death moan, or sound of "last breath." These three seasoned hunters of dangerous animals will not approach too closely until certain the animal cannot stand and attack.

The three hunters stood around the bear all thinking the same. Look at the thickness of the fur, the size of it, the claws, the foot pads, the amount of meat they will have. As Crow and Cree began skinning to later butcher the bear meat, Koda built a large fire. This thick bear fur skin is going to be very warm to have as a cover some cold dark season night.

After enjoying the taste of fire charred bear roast, the hunters would stay the night, packing their kill back to camp the next day. Laying down to sleep for the night, Cree thought proudly how Koda had not wavered when the bear charged Crow. How Koda stepped in and speared the wounded bear.

Being drawn by the campfire and the smell of meat they watched the hunters from a distance. They would wait for daylight before going any closer.

CHAPTER FOURTEEN
Ice People

They took bear claws for Koda and Pawee to necklace and leg tendons for cord and bow strings. Bear skin and meat, all was packed and ready for the trip back to camp. Touching Crow on the shoulder, Cree pointed to the north. Five figures in the distance were walking towards the hunters. Approaching closer, Cree could see four men, one female. These people were of smaller stature, short with thick bodies. All wearing fur clothing, pull up fur headwear attached over their coats, and superior footwear and leggings. These people were dressed for the cold of the north.

The hunters watched the approach cautiously with bows at ready. The leader approached with one hand raised above head with palm forward, extending the other hand holding what appeared to be dry-cured fish. Crow and Cree took this as a sign or a token of goodwill and peace. Coming much closer, the five strangers were invited to stand by the fire by Crow's hand jesters. With no common spoken language, they wondered of each other and used only hand sign. Uttering Yupi over and over while tapping his chest with both hands, the hunters understood him as leader and name.

Doing the same for each member, the hunters learned the names of three brothers, Aput, Amaru, and Kanaa. Yupi, the leader, pointed at the girl, saying Akira, his daughter, the sister of the brothers. The five were offered cooked meat from last night's meal. Nodding their thanks, they were obviously hungry for red meat. They carried smaller bow and arrows, not suitable for large game, and had but only one spear. Their knives were of sharpened larger white bone (whale bone). Strapped to their side each man carried solid white bone carved into the shaped of handheld clubs.

Using his words and hand sign, Yupi told the story of his family to the hunters. Crow seemed to understand through Yupi's words and hand sign. When speaking of forest, he would point and repeat in his language. It became known he and Crow were connecting and could communicate with each other. Yupi went on, explaining their homeland was far to the west of the crossing. They came from a northern land of ice and cold. A land of many family bands living on the ice, hunting whale, and seal. For generations the people had hunted and lived on the ice. The cold became more cold and the ice pushed farther into the sea. The ice packs had become so vast, it became more and more difficult to find seal or walrus.

With less seal, walrus, or sea to hunt, the time came to search for new homeland. Yupi's family, along with another did go in search of new ice to hunt. Crossing the land bridge, the fellow group left to go north for the ice and sea to hunt and live. Yupi and family continued on seeking less ice, more sea and inland rivers to hunt and live. In search of such land, their hunting techniques, tools, and weapons would need to improve and change to be successful in this land. Yupi and family wished to join with a family of hunters to better understand survival in this land.

Invited to follow they helped pack and carry take back to home camp of Crow's hunters. Yupi's three sons followed with carried packed meat, Akira walked along with her father. Arriving at Crow's camp, Yupi and family saw a large campfire, two animal-skin-covered huts, and animal skins staked to dry in the sun. There were fish and meat stuck to poles hung over the fire to smoke and dry. They saw animal tendons stretched tight between two standing poles to dry into raw hide for strapping, stitching, and bowstring. Stone bowls held berries and nuts, and many tools, spears, and arrows. Crow and Cree agreed Yupi's family could hunt and live side by side with them. With six or seven hunters, they could hunt for more, and larger game animals for food and skins.

As Yupi and sons worked with Crow, Cree, and Koda getting the skin, meat bone, and sinew unpacked. Crow motioned for Yupi to follow, taking him a short distance, showing where he should make shelters for his family camp. Yupi and sons began spreading skins over brush for sleeping shelter. They made fire and began to set up camp, laying out their hunting weapons, dried food, skins, and tools.

The next day the three hunters have Yupi and sons follow to a stream for water, guide them to trees for limbs or branches to use for constructing huts to be covered with skins for permanent shelters. Akira would work with Pawee to learn her methods of scraping and curing skins. Akira's family used smaller and less powerful bows, she would learn of twisting sinew and tendons for bowstring. How to make strapping and rawhide cord from narrow strips of hide. Being from living in a land of ice and harsh cold, Akira knew well of making and stitching of clothing or footwear. Akira would teach Pawee in making fur-lined hoods to be pulled up over hunters' head in the cold.

Pawee was patient and would teach and mentor Akira well. It was unknown to Pawee of Akira's mother having been killed when attacked by an ice bear. Yupi had taken his sons hunting, leaving behind a very young Akira and her mother. Knowing she and Akira were being stalked, the mother covered the child in snow and ice leaving just enough of an opening for air. Telling the young Akira to remain quiet and no movement, the mother then scented herself with rubbed on seal fat and ran far from the child. She knew the bear would follow her scent of seal.

The bear not scenting the child, remained tracking the mother, overtaking her far from the child's hiding place. Late in the day, returning from the hunt, Yupi found no fire or family. He and sons began following tracks before finding the child still hidden in the snow. The hunters with child went on following tracks of the woman when they saw she was followed by the bear. Darkness had fallen, and following tracks would not be possible. Protecting his young daughter was his most important responsibility. Taking the girl and sons back to camp, Yupi built a fire of whale blubber inside a small ice hut covered in animal skins. Feeding themselves and the child, they slept with bows and knives at ready.

Next morning Yupi had the brothers stay to protect Akira while he followed tracks, looking for their mother. A far walking distance from camp he found the site of the bear attack on the mother. Everything Yupi found of the attack was as he feared. He gathered the mother's clothing and remains, wrapping it in a bundle of his coat and setting it on fire. Watching the burning fire, Yupi chanted words in song to her spirit. Yupi found a necklace of miniature ice animals carved from whale bone among her clothes. He kept the necklace to give Akira when she was older.

Crow showing Yupi the size difference in their hunting bows gave the message of Yupi's family making larger bow and arrows. Cree and Koda taught and helped the brothers make axes with handles from wood and sharpened flint or mineral rock heads. Showed how to attach the axe head to handle with water-soaked rawhide strips tied tightly, allowing to shrink even more tight and strong after drying. Pawee would teach Akira to make powerful bow string from bear leg tendons. She also was teaching Akira to make precision arrow shafts with bird feather guides. Arrow shafts made by Pawee would fly straight for the hunter. Most hunters preferred making and sharpening their own flint arrowheads.

Akira was learning much from Pawee. Without a mother to guide her, Akira was giving more time learning more survival and hunting skills from her brothers and father.

After several days of more new skills, the Yupi family now had two shelter huts and their own campsite. Yupi and sons were ready to hunt with their new weapons. Now having seven hunters, Crow announced they would bison hunt together.

CHAPTER FIFTEEN
Bison Hunters

Finding a small herd of grazing bison, Cree, Koda, and Aput would hunt with spears, driving the bison forward. One hunter to each side and one pushing the rear running alongside to steer the bison's direction. Crow, Yupi, Amaru, and Kanaa would hunt with bow and arrows. They would be ahead, two on each side, hidden in brush and waiting for the bison being so close before stepping out. After finding a group of bison, the three drivers would wait for the bow hunters to go ahead and become hidden from the bison. The drivers crouched on hands and knees, covered themselves with bison fur skins and crept into position. The drivers planned to get as close as possible to not alert the bison before standing with spears and running the bison towards the four hunters.

With the hunters running along yelling and poking with spears, the bison ran to the bowhunters' position. Once in range, the four hunters shot arrows into the lead bison. At the same time the running hunters speared bison. Each hunter shot two or three arrows, leaving three bison dead on the ground. The spear hunters killed one bison for a total of four. This was Crow's most successful bison hunt. There would be enough bison meat and skins for the two families to share. The two families began in the work of skinning and butchering the bison.

Now back at camp there was much to be done by all—smoking bison meat to preserve; scraping and staking hides to sun dry; stretching and curing tendons and sinew; cleaning and sharpening arrowheads and knives; and finally building a large fire for celebrating the bison hunt. As they worked, Pawee taught Akira the names of her family, Akira had done the same teaching Pawee.

After darkness both families sat around the fire charring bison meat for the celebration feast. Akira made a drink of crushed wild grapes and berries for all to enjoy. Aput turned and told Yupi, "We are being watched from the trees. It walks softly but carries a strong odor." Aput was the gifted hunter of their family. He understood the ways and balance of the wilderness. Aput had been a great whale hunter and builder of boats in his homeland. Aput carried no fear.

It had watched from the trees, careful not to be seen or heard. The hunters sat surrounding and staring into fire. It saw the two hunters stop and look towards where it stood. It had seen them before walking through the forest. Silently it backed away, turned, and walked quietly deeper into the darkness.

CHAPTER SIXTEEN
"Sumon"

Aput and Koda were the same age, sharing several skills needed of successful hunters. Making and using tools for hunting all game, large and small. Trapping, tracking, and stalking game animals. Aput told Koda about his feelings of their being watched the previous night. Aput wanted to look for tracks or signs of who may be watching. Going to the area Aput suspected they were watched, no tracks or sign of any were found.

Nearby is a river stream with fast running current. It is fed from mountain snow and rain runoff, growing as it flows downstream. Smaller forest streams feed into the larger carrying fallen insects and nutrients from the floor of the forest. The main larger rocky stream carries all the tributary runoff father down, through rapids, cascades, and falls. Eventually this shallow small stream becomes greater ending its journey by emptying all it carries into the sea.

This stream, as with most streams, current can be heard running through the rapids and cascades. Hearing this, Koda and Aput walked in that direction to scoop up a drink of cool water. As the two came to the water, Aput began to shout, "Sumon, sumon, sumon," pointing to the cascades. Not understanding Aput's language, Koda stood wondering what was spoken, when at that moment Koda saw movement in the cascades. It was a moving mass of fish just below the water's surface, all swimming in unison—upstream. As the fish approached the falls, beautiful fish began leaping from the water to move up the downward flow of current, up and over the falls. Each fish finding a starting position, awaiting its turn to leap and swim up the rapids. This was the run of the salmon (sumon).

After spawning and hatching from eggs, the young salmon (alevin) begins a journey in distance and life stages. During its first year, evolving to a fry, to a smolt, the salmon will be moving farther downstream from its birthplace to the sea. Once near the ocean, salmon begin to transform into the anatomy from a freshwater fish to a saltwater salmon. The gills and kidneys undergo change to process saltwater, along with a body coloring change to that of a deep-water fish. Depending on salmon species, they may stay at sea two to seven years until fully matured and are driven to return to their place of birth. Having the strength to endure the last stage of their journey, natural instinct will guide them to their final destination. Reaching the very pool where they were born, they will spawn, nature ending their life to begin anew.

Koda and Aput stood watching this amazing act of nature's empowering this species to transform itself in order to return to their ancient spawning pools. After spawning, the mature salmon will have completed their life cycle. They will die and bodies decay in the same pools where they started life. Salmon decaying bodies will serve to feed the other wildlife of the wilderness.

The migrating fish were more than plentiful. Aput had seen this before south of his polar homeland. The salmon did not feed when migrating to their spawning grounds. To catch them you could do with traps, spears, or your hands by standing in shallow cascades or beside the falls.

Aput motioned to Koda he was going to camp to get his brothers and father, Yupi. Koda stood in shallows as the salmon swam around his feet. He scooped up and in one motion tossed onto the stream bank. Gutting and cleaning his catch with a sharp knife, he cut out a portion of the filet for himself. This was nature's provision of energy in the form of calories and nutrients for man and animal. Aput brought back both families, and they all began catching a bonanza of salmon. Even Keme joined the fun, eating the gutted fish pile on the ground.

Cooked over fire, eaten raw, smoked, or dried in the sun, they could be preserved to be eaten much later. Once gutted, the fish could be fileted, leaving the two sides connected to the tail. Taking a strong tree limb and placing it between two poles, the fish were hung over the limb to dry. Or a fire could be placed underneath and allowed to smoke the filets. It was wonderful food for both families. Yupi and family believed in celebrating the gifts of the wilderness. There would be a large fire tonight with a great meal of salmon for all.

Koda saw that Aput and family traditions were much more spiritual, their celebrating with tribal chants and singing to the spirits of the wilderness for the gifts of life. They celebrated the whales, the seal, the gift of fire, and the warmth of the green season. This had been an exciting day for both families. Crow's would let the fire burn slowly down and sleep in their huts. Crow and Koda shared a hut, Cree and Pawee the other. Laying on his bison fur bedding, Koda listened to the faraway howl of wolves. Koda also thought of the three boulder territory markers wondering of the tales of the ancient Others. Why have they never been seen in the forest. Were the creatures he had seen the Others? He thought they were.

Koda thought more of going south, through and over the mountains. Would they find the plains of grazing animals, spread across the plains as far as a human could see? You could have your own territory to hunt and live. The cold dark season would not last as harsh, the green season would last much longer. Yes, this is what Koda will do, see more of this new land.

CHAPTER SEVENTEEN
White Goats

Yupi's people were and are of a cold weather existence. They are a nomadic people, migrating with the changing seasons. His people were ice and sea hunters. Through ages those were rugged people who would follow the ice packs hunting walrus, seal, and whale. Hunting seal was done over ice floes or open water. Walrus liked more of a solid rocky beach when leaving the water. Whale hunting was more open-water hunting. Yupi's ancestors were master whale hunters and boat builders

Yupi as a young boy had watched his father and other hunters whale hunt. As he grew older, he was more with the hunters and began learning about seal and whale hunting. Yupi enjoyed working with the hunters when building whale boats. Whale bone was gathered from remains of previous hunts or remains that had washed ashore. First to build was the frame of the boat. Gathering straight and curved rib bone. Using straight bone for the keel, a single long bone up to 20′, gave the foundation and strength for the structure. The rib bones were used for strength and stability of the sides. Yupi learned to lash the ribs and keel bone together using wet strips of seal or walrus skin.

As the wet skin dried, the joints of bone would be strong enough to withstand pounding ocean waves. Straight bone for top rail support was lashed to ribs in the same manner. Finally, seal or walrus skin was stretched across the frame, also attached to the rails with lashing. The skin of the whale boat was waterproofed with seal oil rubbed over the entire outer layer and seams. Yupi was taken out on the ice by his father and shown how to build an ice shelter from cutting blocks of ice. It came to be Yupi learned hunting from going, watching, and being with hunters. When hunters sat and had their meals, Yupi listened to the stories of past hunts. He practiced making hunting tools and weapons. When his time came to join his father on hunts, he was ready to be like his father. Yupi eventually became a hunter and leader of their group of people.

Being of ice climate, cold weather people, Yupi knew of important methods for survival on the ice that are provided by nature. Ways of survival hunters use on ice or land.

Crow and Yupi were teaching family the clever acquired knowledge of nature and the wilderness. The wise seek, see, and listen to learn the use of knowledge. The same as they were taught, so had Crow and Yupi taught their sons, and so were doing even now.

Living high in the mountains throughout the season were groups of white mountain goats. Sure-footed to live, walk, climb, feed along the high cliffs and ledges of the mountains. Yupi and his sons would go to the mountains to hunt and see the white goats of the cliffs. Akira would stay with Pawee while her hunters were away.

The wooly fur of these animals was double insulated to withstand the bitter cold and winds of the high mountains in cold season. Having an inner layer of fine dense wool fur covered by an outer layer of longer hollow hair. This being the reason they would hunt the dangerous cliffs. The insulated goat skins Akira would make into cold weather and waterproof clothing for her family. This wilderness provides much abundance for the hunter who seeks and sees. The tundra and valleys with bison and caribou, forest of elk and deer. There is no want for game, food, and skins for shelter. Packing dried meats, fish, bedding and hunting weapons, the hunters began their long trek to and up the mountains in search of white goat.

Reaching the base of the mountains, the hunters had to work their way up to the tree line. As if the mountain had shed itself of unwanted rock and shale, it left a difficult climb for the hunters to ascend. With loose rock and shale underfoot, it was difficult and tedious to work up the mountainside. The loose rock did hide a secret pleasure—moths. Seeking warmth and rest, they would get under the rocks for shelter and the warmth from the rock soaking up the sunlight. Finding a juicy plump moth for a hunter's snack of calories and energy. Caution was necessary as bears also knew of and would come browse the rocks for moths. Yupi and Aput had hunted mountains, though never to the height of the white goats. Aput's brothers, Kanaa and Amaru, had also never hunted the mountain heights.

Going higher, the hunters found a rocky plateau where they could quietly watch for any movement of white goats. Goats living in the mountains are a very elusive animal. The sense of smell of the white goat is not it's primary defense against predators. The ability to move, run, leap ledge to ledge, walk cliff edges, to go where no predator or hunter can follow and excellent eyesight are why they are an elusive animal. The goats' eyesight is such a keen protective mechanism it can spot any minor movement. Because of the goat's ability to move about its environment, it cannot be run down by predators, rather it must be stalked and ambushed.

As they continued watching the mountainside, Yupi told his plan to hunt the goats. Once the goats are seen, Yupi and Aput will slowly move back from this position, then go higher to circle and move in front of the goats from a higher position. Hopefully the goats will approach the unseen hunters from a lower position. The hunters using bows and arrows, would shoot down on the white goats. The hunters continued their vigilant watch for goats; however, at this elevation, clouds, fog, and light snow limited visibility. With changing weather for the worse, Yupi decided they would all spend the night on the mountain. It would be too dangerous to attempt getting to a lower elevation in dark and foggy conditions. Deciding to stay on the plateau the hunters found a rock overhang they could shelter under for the night. They packed some fur skins for bedding and warmth, but would have no fire for lack of wood or other material to burn at this elevation.

The four hunters crowded under the overhang, ate some dried bison meat, and covered with fur skins for warmth. As night fell, they heard distant howling cries and yelping. It was an unknown howling, not wolves or panthers. Soon after, large rocks, shale, and small boulders began coming over the ledge from above. Maybe white goats walking above, or bear. Yupi did not think so. Someone did not want them on the mountain. Yupi had been told stories of mountain people, of men with no hair and with drawing on their bodies and face. They were an aggressive and unnatural people. Perhaps Yupi and the hunters had come upon the territory of such people on this mountain.

At early light, the hunters would leave the plateau, descend the mountain, and hunt white goat another day. The howling, yelps, and falling rocks stopped later during that night. Returning to camp, the hunters did kill, skin, and butcher a caribou, taking it back to camp, where they explained to Crow and Cree of bad weather and no white goats found. No mention of any other.

CHAPTER EIGHTEEN
Silent Woods

Searching for deer, Aput and his brothers crossed the valley looking for unknown forest never known to be hunted. Packed to spend days away from camp, armed with bows, arrows, and spears, the hunters walked two days until finding new forest. Clean crisp air, green forest, the three were ready for new adventure. They had long been guided through the heritage of their people to honor and respect the wilderness. Learned to appreciate the abundance of wildlife, to hunt and kill only for food and shelter. These hunters will honor this new forest as such, perhaps being the first and only to hunt this forest. Being thick with large old evergreens, pine, and brushy shrub, it was a dark forest. Desirable with protective cover for quarry animals such as elk, deer along with forest bison. Wildlife could live under the safety of dense greenwood.

Aput would lead his brothers through the forest seeking game trails and a suitable camp area. They found a clean fresh-water stream and followed its flow deeper into the woods. Many long ago fallen trees covered with decay and moss made walking over or around necessary. Finding a small opening near the stream, the hunters dropped packs, sat back resting before setting up a hunting camp. Aput decided no fire for now. Smoke would alert the keen scent sense of deer to their presence. Before darkness Aput wanted to search for tracks and trails of deer. He went one direction, sending his two brothers together in another. When going through unknown woods, travelers need to mark their trail, paying attention to sign for direction back to their starting point.

Aput's first sign is the sound of the stream. Listening for a repetitive sound is a significant sign. Aput would mark fallen trees by scraping moss, indicating the "from" direction. Taking three longer tree limbs and standing crossed at top as a tripod was good to be seen from a distance. Taking large rocks and stacking two or three is another useable sign to find direction. Even the most experienced hunter can become directional lost in deep forest if care is not given to using natural signs. Aput did find deer tracks and game trails, which encouraged his hopes for successful hunting. Going back to camp, Aput quickly heard the sound of the stream. He had also marked fallen trees. Arriving at camp before his brothers, and with coming darkness, he became concerned.

Amaru and Kanaa had gone in a different direction, crossing the stream and going deeper into this forest. What they found was a dark, quiet, still forest. It had a smell of dark decay. Noticeably not seeing any birds or small animals as squirrels, rabbit, or rodents. There were no animals sounds, elk calls, wolves' howls, screeching birds. Something was not right. It is time to be alert, they told each other. Continuing to walk farther into the woods, they found a fallen tree with one large stream boulder placed on it. How would a rounded obvious stream rock this size be on a fallen tree? Going farther, they found no trails, together with very few deer or elk tracks. This area was almost a dead forest. Living plant life but not wildlife.

Going on, the two walked up to the skeleton remains of what they thought to be an elk. The head had been removed. Close by Kanaa found charred wood, some stones of what appeared to be an older fire site. There were some footprints around the site. Kanaa and Amaru were not the first in this forest. The fire site was cold and muddy, indicating it had been sometime since last used. Kanaa felt they should go no farther into the forest, best to quietly return to their camp. Aput needed to be alerted. They had marked their trail into the forest, finding the direction back, they made effort to cover their trail and remove any sign of their presence, taking dirt and twigs to cover moss scrapings from fallen trees or stones placed along the return trail.

Kanaa and Amaru had gone much deeper into the forest, and darkness was coming quickly; they could not hesitate. If not, the two would stay the night away from camp. This is not where they wanted to be without Aput. Kanaa took hold of Amaru's wrist as if to stop him and shushed him from making any sound. Kanaa could hear the whistling signals from behind them. He also could sense movement but too far back to see through the dark. They had been discovered and were being followed. Kanaa wondered, *have we crossed into someone's territory? Who would live in such a forest? Were they peaceful people?*

No chance should be taken. Peaceful people would have called out to intruders. In the darkness, Kanaa motioned to Amaru to follow. Finding a large fallen tree, the two crept down on the backside, pushing as closely to under the fallen tree as possible. They would remain here and move no farther until not being followed. Seeing or hearing no movement, nor whistling signals, Kanaa knew not to move. Kanaa and Amaru would stay in place.

Much of the night had passed and still no sounds of followers. Kanaa was sure they were followed for some distance. The sounds stopped when he and Amaru hid. The followers had also stopped, waiting to see movement of the intruders.

Aput at camp began building a fire, a large fire after deciding his brothers were lost or had some trouble. If lost, the fire may lead them to the campsite. Throwing more wood on the fire, Aput with bow and arrows stepped back into the darkness not knowing what beast the fire may also attract. From where they hid, Kanaa could see the distant flicker of Aput's fire. The followers also saw the fire. In the darkness, Kanaa could not see the followers, only hear the sound of their moving towards Aput's fire.

As the followers came closer to Aput, he heard more than two moving in his direction. Aput stepped back farther so as not to be seen in the light of the fire. Momentarily he saw figures of people through the light of fire; they were still in the edge of the woods. He could see their faces and heads were painted with white stripes and symbols. The same covering their arms. Kanaa and Amaru came from their hiding, following from behind the painted people. Two of the painted people had stayed hidden, waiting for the intruders to move towards the fire. Still in darkness, Kanaa did not know of them until they were on Amaru with knives and clubs. Kanaa turned with bow in hand and released an arrow into one of the attackers.

Running to Amaru, he released another arrow, killing the second attacker. Kanaa was not soon enough to save Amaru. He had been stabbed and beaten with a club. Thinking of the danger for his brother Aput, Kanaa ran towards the fire of camp. Aput still unseen took aim and began shooting arrows into painted people near the fire. Three fell to the ground before the others backed out returning to the darkness of the trees. Some began shooting arrows towards Aput. Kanaa, coming from behind, hit two with arrows. The remaining few called out to each other and began moving away from the camp back into the forest.

Giving the painted time to move back through the forest, Aput and Kanaa went back for their fallen brother, Amaru, killed by the painted people. They would carry Amaru to near the stream. There the two covered him, bows, arrows, and his knives with rocks and stones to honor him as a hunter. The rocks were to respect and protect Amaru's spirit from scavenging wildlife. Kanaa wondered what to do with the painted people bodies.

Aput said, "We will not honor them. They died as killers to be disrespected. We will dishonor them by building a large fire, burning them, leaving to be eaten by the worms. We will be the enemy of the painted people, their children, and children's children will be enemy. When hunting them, we, too, will wear painted faces and kill them with our arrows. As they did our brother, Amaru, we shall do them. Let us now return to our father and sister."

CHAPTER NINETEEN
Wolves and Lions

Crow, leaving camp, walked for the stream, looking for flint suitable for arrowheads. Finding and walking upstream for part of a day, he would fish and look for flint. Going farther, he began to find washed-downstream flint. Shooting with arrow a fish from the stream, he sat to fire build and have his fish. Afterwards he lay back on the sun-warmed bank of the stream. With arms folded under his head Crow watched the white clouds and blue sky. A cool breeze blew across his face, sending him to close his eyes and rest. He thought of when he was a young boy, of his father and grandfather.

Eight wolves in a pack had stalked and separated from a group a young female bison and her recent born calf. Wolves can be magnificent hunters. Hunting as a social group they will identify, and single out a target from a group or herd. This young female bison had defended herself and calf, but was eventually no match for the wolf pack. She and her calf fell to the wolves. Announcing success, howling and calling in members of the family to share in their turn.

Hearing this, Crow stood and let curiosity lead him to the wolves' excitement. From a very cautious position, Crow watched the pack on the bison, before deciding he should leave. Too many wolves and danger to be here. Unfortunately, the late-coming wolf family came upon Crow. Instantly knowing his danger, he dropped all he carried and began up a tree. He kept his bow and sheathed arrows strapped to his back. He was up a safe distance before the wolves reached the tree base. They howled and yelped to alert the feeding pack. After their fill of bison, the pack gathered around the tree. Patiently, the pack watched Crow, then decided to relax. Laying down, they are going to wait for the hunter.

With darkness coming, Crow was thinking he could be in a bad predicament. High in a tree, no food, no water, and a pack of wolves daring him to come down. As night fell over the forest, the wolves began their howling. Continuing to wait at the base of the tree, the wolves showed no sign of leaving. Crow found a fork of thick branches he could settle down in to sleep without much danger of falling. Crow awoke later, still night, noticing the silence. Not hearing any sound of wolves, he was not going to come down before daybreak. Crow knew better than to be tricked by cunning wolves. Sunlight and no wolves to be seen. *Why did they leave?*

As if it matters to Crow's situation could not be any worse than a pack of wolves, two very large lions lay sleeping at the base of his tree. Hearing the commotion of the wolves, the two hunting lions came to investigate. Claiming the bison remains for themselves, the lions also claimed the tree and the hunter up the tree. The wolves wisely left, no match for two lions over 650 pounds each. The two lions laying on backs with bison full bellies facing up, Crow thought they looked almost completely harmless. Crow, assessing his problem, knew the heavy large lions were not tree climbers. Nothing to be done, only patience.

Finally, one lion wakes, does his stretching to loosen muscle, stands looking about, and looking up to be sure Crow is still in the tree. This lion wanders to the stream for water and to the bison remains, not hungry, only to warn off vultures. The second lion wakes, looks up at Crow and snarls a good-morning growl.

Being not at camp, Crow did not want Cree and Koda to come searching for him only to stumble upon these lions. If only an elk or caribou, should come within distance and draw the attention of the lions, while away Crow could come down and escape unnoticed. Lions are not going to be patient for long. They are hunters and will soon be looking for prey. Crow himself was becoming thirsty, hungry, also was tired and restless of the tree.

Back at camp Koda and Cree spoke of Crow's not being there. Each knew he searched for flint, which would not be unusual for him to be away overnight. Perhaps Crow went farther than intended; tonight he should return. Koda and Cree were each becoming restless, they were ready to continue their journey to the south. To see the other side of the mountains, what lands would open up to them, what wildlife?

Looking towards the sun and shadows it cast told Crow the day was short and darkness was coming. Persistent lions remained at the tree, looking up at Crow as they took turns at the bison remains. Tonight, would be for Crow another of misery in this tree. Lions prefer fresh meat, perhaps after dark they will hunt. Crow would be watching and listening, if lions leave, Crow was coming down. Watching before dark, both lions stood and stretched from their nap. As darkness fell the large male raised his forward body and front paws onto the side of the tree. Digging his claws into the tree bark and raking down, claws were sharpened.

When finished the second lion did the same. The two were now primed to night hunt for fresh meat. Crow watched every move they made and listened for any sign they had left the tree. Crow watched and waited. Long after he came down with bow and arrow and began to move quietly toward home camp. After a safe long distance from the tree, he climbed another to stay the night. Too dangerous to night walk an unknown forest alone.

So, it came to be as darkness came, wolf Keme went seeking his adopted parent Crow. Having been away from camp for days and nights, Keme began following Crow's scent trail. Keme well knew the human scent of Crow.

During a time long ago in the homeland, hunters came across Keme's mother and her pups' dugout. Protecting her family, the hunters killed the mother wolf. Hearing the yelping pups, hunters began pulling them out and smashing them against a tree. Wolves were competition and threats to humans. Crow reached in and pulled out the last pup, eyes barely open Crow pushed the pup down into his coat. That was Keme's first scent of Crow. Taking back to camp, the two have hunted and been together since.

Following his scent for most of the night, Keme came to a tree with a dangerous scent. The scent of lions, with scent of Crow going on through the forest. Keme followed. Coming to a tree where the scent stopped, Keme sat, wagged his tail, looked up the tree and whined. Waking, Crow could hear but could not see Keme in the darkness. "Is that you?" Crow called. Whining, yelping, wagging the tail, Crow knew, and down the tree he came. Waiting for daylight, they sat at the tree, side by side.

After daybreak the two found their way to home camp and received a hearty welcome from all.

CHAPTER TWENTY
Akira

It came that Crow and Cree accepted this, their home camp, to become their home camp for a while. It matched their needs of food sources, shelter, and climate. Crow and Cree wanted this land of mountains, valleys of grazing land, forest, streams, and rivers for their new home. Koda had the pull of exploring, finding the other side of the mountains, going on south!

Both wanted to build a larger and more moveable shelter to replace their current small huts. In their previous homeland, some people built shelters using multiple longer, shaped poles made from sturdy young trees. Placing the poles on the ground, you then using rawhide tied the narrow end of each pole tightly together. Then, taking the structure of poles, standing up, forming a broad circular base of the poles being evenly spaced, the narrow tied together end forming the top. The result is a structure with a broad base and narrow closed top. Covered with animal hides, the shelter would have steep sides for shedding heavy snowfall or rain. The hides at the top could be flapped open or closed allowing for smoke from fire to exit, or preventing rain or snow entering when closed. Crow and Cree would begin cutting poles for their first shelter. Yupi was still to decide if his family would stay or continue on.

Pawee and Akira's relationship had become as close friends. Akira was tutored in the ways of camp life. Pawee could hope for Akira becoming heart mate for Koda. The two had come to spend more time together. Akira especially liked fishing with Koda. He was an excellent fisherman, teaching her trapping fish, and catching using very thin strips of twisted animal skin and hooks cut from bone. Koda had taught Akira the use of bow and arrow. Akira was common in hunting small game with Koda. She felt very safe when with Koda, she wanted someday they to be together.

Unknown to Pawee, Koda was thinking the same of Akira. She was his age, attractive to him, he much enjoyed being with her, as well he thought she enjoyed being with him. When the families gathered around the fire during darkness, Koda took notice Akira would find a sitting place beside him.

CHAPTER TWENTY-ONE
Picking Berries

This was the season of berries—blueberry, cranberry, crowberry, and raspberry. Pawee and Akira would go pick berries each day. Berries were a favorite eaten fresh, Pawee also would dry the berries in sunlight and use cold season as a flavor for hot drink. When out picking berry, Pawee and Akira would normally stay close to camp, but with this being the season of all varieties, they would need to hunt around camp and into the edge of the forest. Koda, usually as today, would go with them or be close by for protection. Today they were picking in the forest, not deep in but far enough for the sunlight to reach in to ripen the fruit.

The other hunters were working together to cut and shape poles for the new shelters. Crow would have two, he and Koda and another for Cree and Pawee. Yupi would build one for he, Akira, Aput, and Kanaa to share.

After finishing the pole cutting and shaping, the men could then strap tie the tops and erect the frame to a size they want. Finally, they would attach animal skins to enclose from weather. Bison hides would be used as ground cover for warm bedding. The very center would be bare ground covered with small rocks and circled by large stones used for fires. The top flap could be open for smoke ventilation when having fire for food or warmth. Koda left berry-picking Pawee and Akira. Leaving Keme behind, Koda went to work with the other hunters. Telling them he would not be gone but a short while and Keme would stay with them.

While forest hunting far from their camp, painted people hunters saw the campfire through the darkness. Moving closer to the forest edge, they came to see the camp of the hunters around their fire. While painted hunters remained deeper in the forest to be unseen, others remained to watch the camps of Crow and Yupi, day and night. As the two women moved deeper in the forest picking berries, Keme continued close to Pawee. Sniffing many unknown scents, he found some scents of special concern. Human scents not of his group. Moving deeper into the woods, Keme could sense the unknowns were close. Wandering farther from the two berry pickers, Keme was on alert, ears erect, turned forward for the slightest sound, eyes seeking any movement. Too close for Keme to react, he caught movement coming directly when he felt the thumps to his side. Two arrows—one going from the side through his heart, the other his lungs. Falling to the soft ground without a whimper, the two pickers never saw or heard that which had just occurred.

The two continued picking berries, putting into a large basket weaved of green vines and twigs. Continuing to look for berries, they drifted farther into the forest, not aware of the presence of danger or of being watched. The three painted hunters allowed the pickers to pass their hidden position as they moved farther away from camp. Pawee, not watching, had gone too far from sight of where they entered the forest. Turning from one direction to another as they looked for more berries, Pawee would eventually find they were lost in a thick forest. Pawee anxiously came to realize Keme was not with them. Asking, Akira also had not seen Keme.

Trying to remain calm, she wanted to convince herself Keme must have gone to be with Crow. Turning in all directions, Pawee felt an insecure weakness. Thinking of lions, wolves, bears, near panic Pawee told Akira, "We are lost." The three painted hunters now between the pickers and their direction to camp stood with bows from hidden positions. Dropping the baskets, Pawee and Akira ran in terror through brush and trees going deeper and deeper in the forest. The painted hunters followed, walking and knowing the two pickers were going the wrong direction.

Being patient, the followers stayed just close enough to continue pushing the two pickers as a hunter would a wounded animal. Running a far distance, Pawee and Akira were tired, thirsty, and could go not much longer. Exhausted, without water, they were down to a staggering walk. The followers were becoming much closer, finally the pickers went no farther and sat down for rest. Now surrounded by the painted hunters, the women had relented to capture. Each woman had her hands tied with rawhide strap and tethered around the neck with the same. With captors leading, holding the tethers, it was made known to the captured any yell or calling would result in knife to the throat.

Moving on in the direction to the captors hunting camp to join the remaining painted hunters. From there they would travel for days to the home camp of the painted people.

CHAPTER TWENTY-TWO
Captives and Searchers

Carrying the last of the poles for the three new shelters, Crow quickly saw Pawee and Akira were not in camp. Asking Koda of where and when of their looking for berries. Strong in everyone's thinking was wild animal attack. Nearing complete darkness, the hunters with bow and arrows stood at forest edge calling for the two. Walking in a short distance, Koda was sure this is the area Pawee and Akira entered searching for berries. Koda remembering, told Crow and Cree of leaving Keme as protection. Too dark for searching, they would stay at forest edge listening for any calls.

At sunrise Pawee and Akira, still tied, were yanked up by tethers. The three captors were joined by perhaps another seven painted hunters. Making every effort to conceal what had been a simple hunters camp from potential searchers, signs of fire were scattered as to not be obvious. Where they had slept was whisked lightly with leafed branches and covered with a scattering of fallen leaves. Having no food, only water, the group moved in a silent, single line at a fast almost trot pace towards their home camp. The two captives tied and in tether were near the front to discourage any sound making or failure to maintain the pace.

At the same time, Crow, Yupi and family begin their search for Pawee and Akira. The hunters spread and slowly walked looking for sign of where the two had been yesterday. First sign found by Cree was berry bushes picked clean. Moving on, they found more of the same; troubling they were still in sight of the forest edge. Crow thinking to himself, *how far into the forest had they gone, why would they go this far, and where is Keme?* Going farther and farther into the forest, Cree thought they were lost, or even worse.

Yupi called out for Crow. Aput and Kanaa came quickly, followed by Crow. With two arrows in his side, there lay Keme. Aput and Kanaa had before seen arrows with three white marks painted on the shafts. "Painted people," they both said. Crow and Cree gazed at each other without a word exchanged. Crow instructed everyone spaced shoulder to shoulder to walk forward looking for any sign. First to find, Koda, seeing a basket with berries spilled out. Tracks found of Pawee and Akira followed by those of three humans. Staying shoulder to shoulder, the hunters moved at the pace of a walk as they made their way through the forest, watching for any sign of Pawee or Akira.

With still a long distance remaining, the captors stopped to eat, rest, and drink cool stream water. Pawee and Akira were allowed to sit, drink water, and rest. The painted hunters were to leave four behind to wait for any following searchers. They would attack any coming for the two women. After the brief rest, they were up and again on their way. As all walked still in a single line, Pawee thought of Cree and Koda, knowing they would be searching for she and Akira. She knew they were hunters who would not stop searching until they found her. She and Akira must be strong, do whatever they must do to survive and wait for family rescue.

Crossing past a three-stacked-boulders warning, captors and captives unknowing, were being watched. It had also come to be known in the world of nature that the painted humans were evil.

CHAPTER TWENTY-THREE
The Rescuers

Four painted hunters staying behind could hear the searchers coming closer through the forest. The hunters remained hidden in brush, waiting for the searchers to come very close. So close the searchers could not quickly react with bows and arrows. The four hunters planned on first shooting arrow, then attacking with hatchets or clubs. The hunters with bows at ready watched as the searchers moved closer and closer. The first arrow went deep into Aput's chest, piercing lung and heart. Yupi, shot through his neck, fell next. Koda's first arrow felled the shooter of Aput. Cree, shot through his upper leg, dropped to the ground. Koda's second arrow dropped the shooter of Yupi. The third hunter's arrow missed Kanaa, so he charged him with his hatchet. As he slashed Kanaa with his hatchet, Crow's arrow went into the back and out the front of the third. The fourth hunter turned and ran falling to his face from Koda's arrow in his back.

Kicking the fourth hunter over with his foot, Koda finished him with an arrow through the chest. Running to his father who had an arrow through his leg, while Crow was helping Kanaa to sit. Yupi and Aput were dead, Cree and Kanaa wounded. Crow would stay behind with Kanaa and Cree who were unable to go further. Koda had a warrior mind-set, going on himself to rescue Pawee and Akira.

Late the Same Day

Before the fall of darkness Koda had walked past the three boulders marking the territory of the Others. After watching the attack of the wolves and the two Others, Koda promised himself he would not go in their territory. This time he had no choice. Going on after darkness, Koda could go no farther. He was tired, could not continue in the dark, and needed to sleep. Later Koda was awakened to distant howls and yelps. He had heard these warnings before. Although being distant, the calls were disturbing and frightening. Koda drew himself against a tree and tried to rest. The howls and yelping stopped; still, there was no way he could sleep. Not knowing if what he heard were the painted people, he would sit and wait for daylight.

After daybreak Koda went on tracking the direction of Pawee and Akira. Going not a long distance, looking ahead, he saw a large dark figure coming through the forest. Stopping no more than twenty steps from the creature, Koda froze, not moving. Staring at Koda was a very large muscular, imposing creature. Covered in dark hair, having black eyes, the creature made no sound. Standing at its side was a smaller, younger, less imposing creature. Both creatures remained silent, showing no expression, or aggression. Still staring at Koda, the two stepped aside. Koda could see Pawee and Akira farther back. Seeing Koda, they ran past the creatures, embracing him. In excitement they begin to tear as they held on to Koda. Watching, the two creatures turned and began to walk back farther into the forest, Koda saw the smaller creature walk away with a pronounced limp in dragging his left foot. Quietly murmuring to himself he knew who these two were.

"Follow me," Koda told his mother and Akira, walking away, not sharing any words until they had passed the three stacked boulders of the creatures' territory. When out of sight of their territory they stopped. Koda had to tell Pawee and Akira of Yupi and Aput being killed, and of the attack by the painted people hunters. He was unsure of how to tell them the story. Adding to the difficulty was Akira not having full understanding of their language. Pawee would have to help explain about Akira's father and brother being dead.

Koda was not sure how and where to start, so he began with the attack by the painted people. Koda went straight to how Yupi and Aput were caught in an ambush and killed by painted people. He carefully explained about Cree and Kanaa being wounded in the same ambush and of still being in the forest and watched by Crow. Hearing all this, Akira buried her head in Pawee's shoulder as they held each other, crying in hurtful pain. Next Koda wanted Pawee to know going about finding them missing from camp, their initial search and they sharing in great anxiety for her and Akira's safety. Koda let them know about being unsure of their being captured up to finding Keme killed and the dropped basket of berries. Koda added very vocally his being afraid he would not see either again and his pain for their safety. Akira held Koda tightly, not speaking after hearing his words.

Koda asked Pawee very few questions about their captors or the creatures. He did ask about the last night, the howls, yelps, and their escape. Pawee and Akira were somewhat quiet about it. Speaking very low Pawee told of the painted hunters stopping to rest and sleep for the darkness. During the night waking to hearing the same as he heard. There was the shaking of trees. They heard large limbs being torn from the trees and thrown into camp. Boulders and large rocks were falling into camp around them. They were surrounded by fierce growls and howls, even so, they did not see any creatures.

Pawee and Akira huddled in the darkness against a large tree. Fearing being struck by either large stone or tree limb, they dared not run. In the darkness she could not see all that was happening, although they heard the screams and calls for help of their captors. The captors were surrounded by a barrage of stones, boulders, parts of trees. Some fell, crushed, some ran into the dark forest, their fate unknown.

As quickly as the violent assault had begun it was over, ending in absolute total silence. Pawee and Akira sat there in the darkness with hands still tied and tethers around the neck. As sunrise came, they saw what remained of the captors' camp. It was as if all had been destroyed by the forest itself. Pawee and Akira stood shaken unsure.

The younger and smaller creature was the first to slowly approach from the forest. Followed by the larger creature, they came to Pawee, to begin unravelling and tear away tied rawhide from her hands. Once her hands were free, she untied Akira and removed the tethers from around their necks. There had been no escape from the captors; they had been rescued. Stepping away the younger stopped, turned, looked directly to Pawee and motioned for the two humans to follow. The large creature led the way all walking in silence, Pawee and Akira being taken to safety.

Now Koda spoke to them about the creatures of the forest. Repeating some of Crows tales of the ancient homeland, the Father of Mountains, and nature's creatures known as the protectors of forest and wildlife. Repeated tales through the ages of these creatures were known to be peaceful and reclusive when undisturbed, staying within their own. Akira never hearing of these stories listened wide-eyed to his words. Koda then went into his story of the wolf attack on the smaller creature, how he was involved and the large creature coming to rescue his younger. Koda telling of not speaking of his encountering the creatures to anyone.

Speaking, Koda said, "Our people are to protect and respect the mystery, solitude, and seclusion of the creatures of the forest. You are to never reveal your knowledge of these creatures. It shall be this down through our children and their children for the ages."

The three walked on to join Crow, Cree, and Kanaa. Crow had cared to their wounds, pulling the arrow from Cree's leg, dressing the bleeding wound with plant leaves. Still some bleeding, Cree was in great pain when attempting to walk. Kanaa had been struck in the chest, arm, and head when attacked by the hatchet-wielding hunter. None of his injuries were dangerous, but Kanaa needed his wounds treated to properly heal. Pawee with protective Koda at her side went finding plants yarrow and goldenrod for treating Cree and Kanaa's wounds. Taking the tops between her hand and rubbing briskly, Pawee gently rubbed on Cree's arrow wounds leaving on to absorb and heal. Akira, watching, did the same for Kanaa's wounds. Staying through the day and night they continued, repeating treating wounds.

Finding a clear place of higher ground, Crow and Koda buried Yupi and Aput side by side under a mound of rocks and stones. Burying with them their prized hunting knives and bows. When done Crow handed Koda a necklace of carved miniature animals of the North Ice. Telling Koda how Yupi had carried this with him, Koda would know when to give to Akira this necklace once belonging to her mother.

The painted hunters killed by Koda and Crow were dragged enough distance from them so as to be not too close to camp. Let the wild beast feast on them.

Three days later, to home camp they walked, slowly, some healing wounds, all thinking of the two left buried in the forest. With a taste of the coming of the cool season in the air, seeing skies gray and cloudy, their thoughts were of past times. Akira, walking side by side with Koda, let her hand touch his, following behind Cree and Pawee smiled. Crow wished for Keme the wolf, how he came to find Crow kept up a tree by lions and wolves. As leader Crow wondered of Akira and Kanaa not having father or brother, to becoming his family.

Koda
One Month Later:

Tonight, the family would celebrate Koda and Akira becoming heart mates. Pawee had worked softening two bear skins to warm the shelter bed of Koda and Akira in the darkness of the cold season. Tonight, would give as celebration gifts. Cree had made a hunting knife from bison horn for the celebration.

Akira crafted a necklace ornamented of bear claws and lion's teeth given to her from Kanaa and Crow. Tonight, she would give it to Koda as a warrior's choker to honor his bravery and manhood. Koda would present to Akira the necklace that had belonged to her mother. He would explain it is a gift from her father, Yupi. Finally, Koda would give her a deer skin coat and boots, his gift made by his mother.

The celebration was an enjoyment of food and drink, the sharing of gifts and all sitting and telling stories of old days and fondness.

At the celebration's end, Koda revealed a decision he had reached. He and Akira would not cross the looming mountain range. Rather they would go east, passing through great forest, once to find grasslands, and turn to the south for a long journey. They would continue south until they found a new homeland of a great wilderness. Koda asked that all family would come with he and Akira.

CHAPTER TWENTY-FOUR

Finding American Wilderness

Months Later:

They all made the journey, came together, passed through the great forest, finding alpine forest, and going on.

Then as if a great passage had opened before them, they found great cliffs of granite reaching to the blue sky. Steaming, bubbling, pools of hot water. Valleys and plains of bison, elk, and deer. It was the wilderness of a new world. They were in their family homeland of generations upon generation to follow.

END